THE ESCAPE OF ARSÈNE LUPIN

Maurice Leblanc

first published in French on January 15, 1906

translated in 1910 by Alexander Teixeira de Mattos

Arsène Lupin had just finished his repast and taken from his pocket an excellent cigar, with a gold band, which he was examining with unusual care, when the door of his cell was opened. He had barely time to throw the cigar into the drawer and move away from the table. The guard entered.

It was the hour for exercise.

"I was waiting for you, my dear boy," exclaimed Lupin, in his accustomed good humor.

They went out together. As soon as they had disappeared at a turn in the corridor, two men entered the cell and commenced a minute examination of it.

One was Inspector Dieuzy; the other was Inspector Folenfant. They wished to verify their suspicion that Arsène Lupin was in communication with his accomplices outside of the prison. On the preceding evening, the 'Grand Journal' had published these lines addressed to its court reporter:

"Monsieur:

"In a recent article you referred to me in most unjustifiable terms. Some days before the opening of my trial I will call you to account. Arsène Lupin."

The handwriting was certainly that of Arsène Lupin. Consequently, he sent letters; and, no doubt, received letters. It was certain that he was preparing for that escape thus arrogantly announced by him.

The situation had become intolerable. Acting in conjunction with the examining judge, the chief of the Sûreté, Mon. Dudouis, had visited the prison and instructed the gaoler in regard to the precautions necessary to insure Lupin's safety. At the same time, he sent the two men to examine the prisoner's cell. They raised every stone, ransacked the bed, did everything customary in such a case, but they discovered nothing, and were about to abandon their investigation when the guard entered hastily and said:

"The drawer.... look in the table-drawer. When I entered just now he was closing it."

They opened the drawer, and Dieuzy exclaimed:

"Ah! we have him this time."

Folenfant stopped him.

"Wait a moment. The chief will want to make an inventory."

"This is a very choice cigar."

"Leave it there, and notify the chief."

Two minutes later Mon. Dudouis examined the contents of the

drawer. First he discovered a bundle of newspaper clippings relating to Arsène Lupin taken from the 'Argus de la Presse,' then a tobacco-box, a pipe, some paper called "onion-peel," and two books. He read the titles of the books. One was an English edition of Carlyle's "Hero-worship"; the other was a charming elzevir, in modern binding, the "Manual of Epictetus," a German translation published at Leyden in 1634. On examining the books, he found that all the pages were underlined and annotated. Were they prepared as a code for correspondence, or did they simply express the studious character of the reader? Then he examined the tobacco-box and the pipe. Finally, he took up the famous cigar with its gold band.

"Fichtre!" he exclaimed. "Our friend smokes a good cigar. It's a Henry Clay."

With the mechanical action of an habitual smoker, he placed the cigar close to his ear and squeezed it to make it crack. Immediately he uttered a cry of surprise. The cigar had yielded under the pressure of his fingers. He examined it more closely, and quickly discovered something white between the leaves of tobacco. Delicately, with the aid of a pin, he withdrew a roll of very thin paper, scarcely larger than a toothpick. It was a letter. He unrolled it, and found these words, written in a feminine handwriting:

"The basket has taken the place of the others. Eight out of ten are ready. On pressing the outer foot the plate goes downward. From twelve to sixteen every day, H-P will wait. But where? Reply at once. Rest easy; your friend is watching over you."

Mon. Dudouis reflected a moment, then said:

"It is quite clear.... the basket.... the eight compartments.... From twelve to sixteen means from twelve to four o'clock."

"But this H-P, that will wait?"

"H-P must mean automobile. H-P, horsepower, is the way they indicate strength of the motor. A twenty-four H-P is an automobile of twenty-four horsepower."

Then he rose, and asked:

"Had the prisoner finished his breakfast?"

"Yes."

"And as he has not yet read the message, which is proved by the condition of the cigar, it is probable that he had just received it."

"How?"

"In his food. Concealed in his bread or in a potato, perhaps."

"Impossible. His food was allowed to be brought in simply to trap him, but we have never found anything in it."

"We will look for Lupin's reply this evening. Detain him

outside for a few minutes. I shall take this to the examining judge, and, if he agrees with me, we will have the letter photographed at once, and in an hour you can replace the letter in the drawer in a cigar similar to this. The prisoner must have no cause for suspicion."

It was not without a certain curiosity that Mon. Dudouis returned to the prison in the evening, accompanied by Inspector Dieuzy. Three empty plates were sitting on the stove in the corner.

"He has eaten?"

"Yes," replied the guard.

"Dieuzy, please cut that macaroni into very small pieces, and open that bread-roll....Nothing?"

"No, chief."

Mon. Dudouis examined the plates, the fork, the spoon, and the knife—an ordinary knife with a rounded blade. He turned the handle to the left; then to the right. It yielded and unscrewed. The knife was hollow, and served as a hiding-place for a sheet of paper.

"Peuh!" he said, "that is not very clever for a man like Arsène. But we mustn't lose any time. You, Dieuzy, go and search the restaurant."

Then he read the note:

"I trust to you, H-P will follow at a distance every day. I will go ahead. Au revoir, dear friend."

"At last," cried Mon. Dudouis, rubbing his hands gleefully, "I think we have the affair in our own hands. A little strategy on our part, and the escape will be a success in so far as the arrest of his confederates are concerned."

"But if Arsène Lupin slips through your fingers?" suggested the guard.

"We will have a sufficient number of men to prevent that. If, however, he displays too much cleverness, ma foi, so much the worse for him! As to his band of robbers, since the chief refuses to speak, the others must."

And, as a matter of fact, Arsène Lupin had very little to say. For several months, Mon. Jules Bouvier, the examining judge, had exerted himself in vain. The investigation had been reduced to a few uninteresting arguments between the judge and the advocate, Maître Danval, one of the leaders of the bar. From time to time, through courtesy, Arsène Lupin would speak. One day he said:

"Yes, monsieur, le judge, I quite agree with you: the robbery of the Crédit Lyonnais, the theft in the rue de

Babylone, the issue of the counterfeit bank-notes, the burglaries at the various châteaux, Armesnil, Gouret, Imblevain, Groseillers, Malaquis, all my work, monsieur, I did it all."

"Then will you explain to me—"

"It is useless. I confess everything in a lump, everything

and even ten times more than you know nothing about."

Wearied by his fruitless task, the judge had suspended his examinations, but he resumed them after the two intercepted messages were brought to his attention; and regularly, at mid-day, Arsène Lupin was taken from the prison to the Dépôt in the prison-van with a certain number of other prisoners. They returned about three or four o'clock.

Now, one afternoon, this return trip was made under unusual conditions. The other prisoners not having been examined, it was decided to take back Arsène Lupin first, thus he found himself alone in the vehicle.

These prison-vans, vulgarly called "panniers à salade"– or salad-baskets–are divided lengthwise by a central corridor from which open ten compartments, five on either side. Each compartment is so arranged that the occupant must assume and retain a sitting posture, and, consequently, the five prisoners are seated one upon the other, and yet separated one from the other by partitions. A municipal guard, standing at one end, watches over the corridor.

Arsène was placed in the third cell on the right, and the heavy vehicle started. He carefully calculated when they left the quai de l'Horloge, and when they passed the Palais de Justice. Then, about the centre of the bridge Saint Michel, with his outer foot, that is to say, his right foot, he pressed upon the metal plate that closed his cell. Immediately something clicked, and the metal plate moved. He was able to ascertain that he was located between the two wheels.

He waited, keeping a sharp look-out. The vehicle was proceeding slowly along the boulevard Saint Michel. At the corner of Saint Germain it stopped. A truck horse had fallen. The traffic having been interrupted, a vast throng of fiacres and omnibuses had gathered there. Arsène Lupin looked out. Another prison-van had stopped close to the one he occupied. He moved the plate still farther, put his foot on one of the spokes of the wheel and leaped to the ground. A coachman saw him, roared with laughter, then tried to raise an outcry, but his voice was lost in the noise of the traffic that had commenced to move again. Moreover, Arsène Lupin was already far away.

He had run for a few steps; but, once upon the sidewalk, he turned and looked around; he seemed

to scent the wind
like a person who
is uncertain which
direction to take.
Then, having decided,
he put his hands in
his pockets, and,
with the careless air
of an idle stroller,
he proceeded up
the boulevard. It
was a warm, bright
autumn day, and the
cafés were full. He
took a seat on the
terrace of one of

them. He ordered a bock and a package of cigarettes. He emptied his glass slowly, smoked one cigarette and lighted a second. Then he asked the waiter to send the proprietor to him. When the proprietor came, Arsène spoke to him in a voice loud enough to be heard by everyone:

"I regret to say, monsieur, I have forgotten my pocketbook. Perhaps, on the strength of my name, you will be pleased to give me credit for a few days. I am Arsène Lupin."

The proprietor looked at him, thinking he was joking. But Arsène repeated:

"Lupin, prisoner at the Santé, but now

a fugitive. I venture to assume that the name inspires you with perfect confidence in me."

And he walked away, amidst shouts of laughter, whilst the proprietor stood amazed.

Lupin strolled along the rue Soufflot, and turned into the rue Saint Jacques. He pursued his way slowly, smoking his cigarettes and looking into the shop-windows. At the Boulevard de Port Royal he took his bearings, discovered where he was, and then walked in the direction of the rue de la Santé. The high forbidding walls of the prison were now before him. He pulled his hat forward to shade his face; then, approaching the sentinel, he asked:

"Is this the prison de la Santé?"

"Yes."

"I wish to regain my cell. The van left me on the way, and I would not abuse—"

"Now, young man, move along—quick!" growled the sentinel.

"Pardon me, but I must pass through that gate. And if you prevent Arsène Lupin from entering the prison it will cost you dear, my friend."

"Arsène Lupin! What are you talking about!"

"I am sorry I haven't a card with me," said Arsène, fumbling in his pockets.

The sentinel eyed him from head to foot, in astonishment. Then, without a word, he rang a bell. The iron gate was partly opened, and Arsène stepped inside. Almost immediately he encountered the keeper of the prison, gesticulating and feigning a violent anger. Arsène smiled and said:

"Come, monsieur, don't play that game with me. What! they take the precaution to carry me alone in the van, prepare a nice little obstruction, and imagine I am going to take to my heels and rejoin my friends. Well, and what about the twenty agents of the Sûreté who accompanied us on foot, in fiacres and on bicycles? No, the arrangement did not please me. I should not have got away alive. Tell me, monsieur, did they count on that?"

He shrugged his shoulders, and added:

"I beg of you, monsieur, not to worry about me. When I wish to escape I shall not require any assistance."

On the second day thereafter, the 'Echo de France,' which had apparently become the official reporter of the exploits of Arsène Lupin,—it was said that he was one of its principal shareholders— published a most complete account of this attempted escape. The exact wording of the messages exchanged between the prisoner and his mysterious friend, the means by which correspondence was constructed, the complicity of the police, the promenade on the Boulevard Saint Michel, the incident at the café Soufflot, everything was disclosed. It was known that the search of the restaurant and its waiters by Inspector Dieuzy had been fruitless. And the public also learned an extraordinary thing which demonstrated the infinite variety of resources that Lupin possessed: the prison-van, in which he was being carried, was prepared for the occasion and substituted by his accomplices for one of the six vans which did service at the prison.

The next escape of Arsène Lupin was not doubted by anyone. He announced it himself, in categorical terms, in a reply to Mon. Bouvier on the day following his attempted escape.

The judge having made a jest about the affair, Arsène was annoyed, and, firmly eyeing the judge, he said, emphatically:

"Listen to me, monsieur! I give you my word of honor that this attempted flight was simply preliminary to my general plan of escape."

"I do not understand," said the judge.

"It is not necessary that you should understand."

And when the judge, in the course of that examination which was reported at length in the columns of the 'Echo de France,' when the judge sought to resume his investigation, Arsène Lupin exclaimed, with an assumed air of lassitude:

"Mon Dieu, Mon Dieu, what's the use! All these questions are of no importance!"

"What! No importance?" cried the judge.

"No; because I shall not be present at the trial."

"You will not be present?"

"No; I have fully decided on that, and nothing will change my mind."

Such assurance combined with the inexplicable indiscretions that Arsène committed every day served to annoy and mystify the officers of the law. There were secrets known only to Arsène Lupin; secrets that he alone could divulge. But for what purpose did he reveal them? And how?

Arsène Lupin was changed to another cell. The judge closed his preliminary investigation. No further proceedings were taken in his case for a period of two months, during which time Arsène was seen almost constantly lying on his bed with his face turned toward the wall. The changing of his cell seemed to discourage him. He refused to see his advocate. He exchanged only a few necessary words with his keepers.

During the fortnight preceding his trial, he resumed his vigorous life. He complained of want of air. Consequently, early every morning he was allowed to exercise in the courtyard, guarded by two men.

Public curiosity had not died out; every day it expected to be regaled with news of his escape; and, it is true, he had gained a considerable amount of public sympathy by reason of his verve, his gayety, his diversity, his inventive genius and the mystery of his life. Arsène Lupin must escape. It was his inevitable fate. The public expected it, and was surprised that the event had been delayed so long. Every morning the Préfect of Police asked his secretary:

"Well, has he escaped yet?"

"No, Monsieur le Préfect."

"To-morrow, probably."

And, on the day before the trial, a gentleman called at the office of the 'Grand Journal,' asked to see the court reporter, threw his card in the reporter's face, and walked rapidly away. These words were written on the card: "Arsène Lupin always keeps his promises."

It was under these conditions that the trial commenced. An enormous crowd gathered at the court. Everybody wished to see the famous Arsène Lupin. They had a gleeful anticipation that the prisoner would play some audacious pranks upon the judge. Advocates and magistrates, reporters and men of the world, actresses and society women were crowded together on the benches provided for the public.

It was a dark, sombre day, with a steady downpour of rain. Only a dim light pervaded the courtroom, and the spectators caught a very indistinct view of the prisoner when the guards brought him in. But his heavy, shambling walk, the manner in which he dropped into his seat, and his passive, stupid appearance were not at all prepossessing. Several times his advocate–one of Mon. Danval's assistants– spoke to him, but he simply shook his head and said nothing.

The clerk read the indictment, then the judge spoke:

"Prisoner at the bar, stand up. Your name, age, and occupation?"

Not receiving any reply, the judge repeated:

"Your name? I ask you your name?"

A thick, slow voice muttered:

"Baudru, Désiré."

A murmur of surprise pervaded the courtroom. But the judge proceeded:

"Baudru, Désiré? Ah! a new alias! Well, as you have already assumed a dozen different names and this one is, no doubt, as imaginary as the others, we will adhere to the name of Arsène Lupin, by which you are more generally known."

The judge referred to his notes, and continued:

"For, despite the most diligent search, your past history remains unknown. Your case is unique in the annals of crime. We know not whom you are, whence you came, your birth and breeding—all is a mystery to us. Three years ago you appeared in our midst as Arsène Lupin, presenting to us a strange combination

of intelligence
and perversion,
immorality and
generosity. Our
knowledge of your
life prior to that
date is vague and
problematical. It
may be that the man
called Rostat who,
eight years ago,
worked with Dickson,
the prestidigitator,
was none other than
Arsène Lupin. It is
probable that the

Russian student who, six years ago, attended the laboratory of Doctor Altier at the Saint Louis Hospital, and who often astonished the doctor by the ingenuity of his hypotheses on subjects of bacteriology and the boldness of his experiments in diseases of the skin, was none other than Arsène Lupin. It is probable, also, that Arsène Lupin was the professor who introduced the Japanese art of jiu-jitsu to the Parisian public. We have some reason to believe that Arsène Lupin was the bicyclist who won the Grand Prix de l'Exposition, received his ten thousand francs, and was never heard of again. Arsène Lupin may have been, also, the person who saved so many lives through the little dormer-window at the Charity Bazaar; and, at the same time, picked their pockets."

The judge paused for a moment, then continued:

"Such is that epoch which seems to have been utilized by you in a thorough preparation for the warfare you have since waged against society; a methodical apprenticeship in which you developed your strength, energy and skill to the highest point possible. Do you acknowledge the accuracy of these facts?"

During this discourse the prisoner had stood balancing himself, first on one foot, then on the other, with shoulders stooped and arms inert. Under the strongest light one could observe his extreme thinness, his hollow cheeks, his projecting

cheek-bones, his
earthen-colored face
dotted with small red
spots and framed in
a rough, straggling
beard. Prison life had
caused him to age
and wither. He had
lost the youthful face
and elegant figure we
had seen portrayed
so often in the
newspapers.

It appeared as if he
had not heard the

question propounded by the judge. Twice it was repeated to him. Then he raised his eyes, seemed to reflect, then, making a desperate effort, he murmured:

"Baudru, Désiré."

The judge smiled, as he said:

"I do not understand the theory of your defense, Arsène

Lupin. If you are seeking to avoid responsibility for your crimes on the ground of imbecility, such a line of defense is open to you. But I shall proceed with the trial and pay no heed to your vagaries."

He then narrated at length the various thefts, swindles and forgeries charged against Lupin. Sometimes he questioned the prisoner, but the latter simply grunted or remained silent. The examination of witnesses commenced. Some of the evidence given was immaterial; other portions of it seemed more important, but through all of it there ran a vein of contradictions and inconsistencies. A wearisome obscurity enveloped the proceedings, until Detective Ganimard was called as a witness; then interest was revived.

From the beginning the actions of the veteran detective appeared strange and unaccountable. He was nervous and ill at ease. Several times he looked at the prisoner, with obvious doubt and anxiety. Then, with his hands resting on the rail in front of him, he recounted the events in which he had participated, including his pursuit of the prisoner across Europe and his arrival in America. He was listened to with great avidity, as his capture of

Arsène Lupin was well known to everyone through the medium of the press. Toward the close of his testimony, after referring to his conversations with Arsène Lupin, he stopped, twice, embarrassed and undecided. It was apparent that he was possessed of some thought which he feared to utter. The judge said to him, sympathetically:

"If you are ill, you may retire for the present."

"No, no, but—"

He stopped, looked sharply at the prisoner, and said:

"I ask permission to scrutinize the prisoner at closer range. There is some mystery about him that I must solve."

He approached the accused man, examined him attentively for several minutes, then returned to the witness-stand, and, in an almost solemn voice, he said:

"I declare, on oath, that the prisoner now before me is not Arsène Lupin."

A profound silence followed the statement. The judge, nonplused for a moment, exclaimed:

"Ah! What do you mean? That is absurd!"

The detective continued:

"At first sight there is a certain resemblance, but if you carefully consider the nose, the mouth, the hair, the color of skin, you will see that it is not Arsène Lupin. And the eyes! Did he ever have those alcoholic eyes!"

"Come, come, witness! What do you mean? Do you pretend to say that we are trying the wrong man?"

"In my opinion, yes. Arsène Lupin has, in some manner, contrived to put this poor devil in his place, unless this man is a willing accomplice."

This dramatic dénouement caused much laughter and excitement amongst the spectators. The judge adjourned the trial, and sent for

Mon. Bouvier, the gaoler, and guards employed in the prison.

When the trial was resumed, Mon. Bouvier and the gaoler examined the accused and declared that there was only a very slight resemblance between the prisoner and Arsène Lupin.

"Well, then!" exclaimed the judge, "who is this man? Where does he come from? What is he in prison for?"

Two of the prison-guards were called and both of them declared that the prisoner was Arsène Lupin. The judged breathed once more.

But one of the guards then said:

"Yes, yes, I think it is he."

"What!" cried the judge, impatiently, "you *think* it is he! What do you mean by that?"

"Well, I saw very little of the prisoner. He was placed in my charge in the evening and, for two months, he seldom stirred, but laid on his bed with his face to the wall."

"What about the time prior to those two months?"

"Before that he occupied a cell in another part of the prison. He was not in cell 24."

Here the head gaoler interrupted, and said:

"We changed him to another cell after his attempted escape."

"But you, monsieur, you have seen him during those two months?"

"I had no occasion to see him. He was always quiet and orderly."

"And this prisoner is not Arsène Lupin?"

"No."

"Then who is he?" demanded the judge.

"I do not know."

"Then we have before us a man who was substituted for Arsène Lupin, two months ago. How do you explain that?"

"I cannot."

In absolute despair, the judge turned to the accused and addressed him in a conciliatory tone:

"Prisoner, can you tell me how, and since when, you became an inmate of the Prison de la Santé?"

The engaging manner of the judge was calculated to disarm the mistrust and awaken the understanding of the accused man. He tried to reply. Finally, under clever and gentle questioning, he succeeded in framing a few phrases from which the following story was gleaned: Two months ago he had been taken to the Dépôt, examined and released. As he was leaving the building, a free man, he was seized by two guards and placed in the prison-van. Since then he had occupied cell 24. He was contented there, plenty to eat, and he slept well—so he did not complain.

All that seemed probable; and, amidst the mirth and excitement of the spectators, the judge adjourned the trial until the story could be investigated and verified.

The following facts were at once established by an examination of the prison records: Eight weeks before a man named Baudru Désiré had slept at the Dépôt. He was released the next day, and left the Dépôt at two o'clock in the afternoon. On the same day at two o'clock, having been examined for the last time, Arsène Lupin left the Dépôt in a prison-van.

Had the guards made a mistake? Had they been deceived by the resemblance and carelessly substituted this man for their prisoner?

Another question suggested itself: Had the substitution been arranged in advance? In that event Baudru must have been an accomplice and must have caused his own arrest for the express purpose of taking Lupin's place. But then, by what miracle had such a plan, based on a series of improbable chances, been carried to success?

Baudru Désiré was turned over to the anthropological

service; they had never seen anything like him. However, they easily traced his past history. He was known at Courbevois, at Asnières and at Levallois. He lived on alms and slept in one of those rag-picker's huts near the barrier de Ternes. He had disappeared from there a year ago.

Had he been enticed away by Arsène Lupin? There was no evidence to that effect. And even if that was so, it did not explain the flight of the prisoner. That still remained a mystery. Amongst twenty theories which sought to explain it, not one was satisfactory. Of the escape itself, there was no doubt;

an escape that was incomprehensible, sensational, in which the public, as well as the officers of the law, could detect a carefully prepared plan, a combination of circumstances marvelously dove-tailed, whereof the dénouement fully justified the confident prediction of Arsène Lupin: "I shall not be present at my trial."

After a month of patient investigation, the problem remained unsolved. The poor devil of a Baudru could not be kept in prison indefinitely, and to place him on trial would be ridiculous. There was no charge against him. Consequently, he was released; but the chief of the Sûrété resolved to keep him under surveillance. This idea originated with Ganimard. From his point of view there was neither complicity nor chance. Baudru was an instrument upon which Arsène Lupin had played with his extraordinary skill. Baudru, when set at liberty, would lead them to Arsène Lupin or, at least, to some of his accomplices.

The two inspectors, Folenfant and Dieuzy, were assigned to assist Ganimard.

One foggy morning in January the prison gates opened and Baudru Désiré stepped forth—a free man. At first he appeared to be quite embarrassed, and walked like a person who has no precise idea whither he is going. He followed the rue de la Santé and the rue Saint Jacques. He stopped in front of an old-clothes shop, removed his jacket and his vest, sold his vest on which he realized a few sous; then, replacing his jacket, he proceeded on his way. He crossed the Seine. At the Châtelet an omnibus passed him.

He wished to enter it, but there was no place. The controller advised him to secure a number, so he entered the waiting-room.

Ganimard called to his two assistants, and, without removing his eyes from the waiting room, he said to them:

"Stop a carriage....
no, two. That will be
better. I will go with
one of you, and we
will follow him."

The men obeyed.
Yet Baudru did not
appear. Ganimard
entered the waiting-
room. It was empty.

"Idiot that I am!" he
muttered, "I forgot
there was another
exit."

There was an interior corridor extending from the waiting-room to the rue Saint Martin. Ganimard rushed through it and arrived just in time to observe Baudru upon the top of the Batignolles-Jardin de Plates omnibus as it was turning the corner of the rue de Rivoli. He ran and caught the omnibus. But he had lost his two assistants. He must continue the pursuit alone. In his anger he was inclined to seize the man by the collar without ceremony. Was it not with premeditation and by means of an ingenious ruse that his pretended imbecile had separated him from his assistants?

He looked at Baudru. The latter was asleep on the bench, his head rolling from side to side, his mouth half-opened, and an incredible expression of stupidity on his blotched face. No, such an adversary was incapable of deceiving old Ganimard. It was a stroke of luck— nothing more.

At the Galleries-Lafayette, the man leaped from the omnibus and took the La Muette tramway, following the boulevard Haussmann and the avenue Victor Hugo. Baudru alighted at La Muette station; and, with a nonchalant air, strolled into the Bois de Boulogne.

He wandered through one path after another, and sometimes retraced his steps. What was he seeking? Had he any definite object? At the end of an hour, he appeared to be faint from fatigue, and, noticing a bench, he sat down. The spot, not far from Auteuil, on the edge of a pond hidden amongst the trees, was absolutely deserted. After the lapse of another half-hour, Ganimard became impatient and resolved to speak to the man. He approached and took a seat beside Baudru, lighted a cigarette, traced some figures in the sand with the end of his cane, and said:

"It's a pleasant day."

No response. But, suddenly the man burst into laughter, a happy, mirthful laugh, spontaneous and irresistible. Ganimard felt his hair stand on end in horror and surprise. It was that laugh, that infernal laugh he knew so well!

With a sudden movement, he seized the man by the

collar and looked at him with a keen, penetrating gaze; and found that he no longer saw the man Baudru. To be sure, he saw Baudru; but, at the same time, he saw the other, the real man, Lupin. He discovered the intense life in the eyes, he filled up the shrunken features, he perceived the real flesh beneath the flabby skin, the real mouth through the grimaces that deformed it. Those were the eyes and mouth of the other, and especially his keen, alert, mocking expression, so clear and youthful!

"Arsène Lupin, Arsène Lupin," he stammered.

Then, in a sudden fit of rage, he seized

Lupin by the throat and tried to hold him down. In spite of his fifty years, he still possessed unusual strength, whilst his adversary was apparently in a weak condition. But the struggle was a brief one. Arsène Lupin made only a slight movement, and, as suddenly as he had made the attack, Ganimard released his hold. His right arm fell inert, useless.

"If you had taken lessons in jiu-jitsu at the quai des Orfèvres," said Lupin, "you would know that that blow is called udi-shi-ghi in Japanese. A second more, and I would have broken your arm and that would have been just what you deserve. I am surprised that you, an old friend whom I respect and before whom I voluntarily expose my incognito, should abuse my confidence in that violent manner. It is unworthy—Ah! What's the matter?"

Ganimard did not reply. That escape for which he deemed himself responsible—was it not he,

Ganimard, who, by his sensational evidence, had led the court into serious error? That escape appeared to him like a dark cloud on his professional career. A tear rolled down his cheek to his gray moustache.

"Oh! mon Dieu, Ganimard, don't take it to heart. If you had not spoken, I would have arranged for some one else to do it. I couldn't allow poor Baudru Désiré to be convicted."

"Then," murmured Ganimard, "it was you that was there? And now you are here?"

"It is I, always I, only I."

"Can it be possible?"

"Oh, it is not the work of a sorcerer. Simply, as the judge remarked at the trial, the apprenticeship of a dozen years that equips a man to cope successfully with all the obstacles in life."

"But your face? Your eyes?"

"You can understand that if I worked eighteen months with Doctor Altier at the

Saint-Louis hospital,
it was not out of
love for the work.
I considered that
he, who would one
day have the honor
of calling himself
Arsène Lupin, ought
to be exempt from
the ordinary laws
governing appearance
and identity.
Appearance? That
can be modified at
will. For instance, a
hypodermic injection

of paraffine will puff up the skin at the desired spot. Pyrogallic acid will change your skin to that of an Indian. The juice of the greater celandine will adorn you with the most beautiful eruptions and tumors. Another chemical affects the growth of your beard and hair; another changes the tone of your voice. Add

to that two months
of dieting in cell 24;
exercises repeated
a thousand times to
enable me to hold
my features in a
certain grimace, to
carry my head at a
certain inclination,
and adapt my back
and shoulders to a
stooping posture.
Then five drops
of atropine in the
eyes to make them

haggard and wild, and the trick is done."

"I do not understand how you deceived the guards."

"The change was progressive. The evolution was so gradual that they failed to notice it."

"But Baudru Désiré?"

"Baudru exists. He is a poor, harmless

fellow whom I met last year; and, really, he bears a certain resemblance to me. Considering my arrest as a possible event, I took charge of Baudru and studied the points wherein we differed in appearance with a view to correct them in my own person. My friends caused him to remain at the Dépôt overnight, and to leave there next day about the same hour as I did—a coincidence easily arranged. Of course, it was necessary to have a record of his detention at the Dépôt in order to establish the fact that such a person was a reality; otherwise, the police would have sought elsewhere to find out my identity. But,

in offering to them
this excellent Baudru,
it was inevitable,
you understand,
inevitable that they
would seize upon
him, and, despite
the insurmountable
difficulties of a
substitution, they
would prefer
to believe in a
substitution than
confess their
ignorance."

"Yes, yes, of course," said Ganimard.

"And then," exclaimed Arsène Lupin, "I held in my hands a trump-card: an anxious public watching and waiting for my escape. And that is the fatal error into which you fell, you and the others, in the course of that fascinating game pending between me and the officers of the law wherein the stake was my liberty. And you supposed that I was playing to the gallery; that I was intoxicated with my success. I, Arsène Lupin, guilty of such weakness! Oh, no! And, no longer ago than the Cahorn affair, you said: "When Arsène Lupin cries from the housetops that he will escape, he has some object in view." But, sapristi, you must understand that in order to escape I must create, in advance, a public belief in that escape, a belief amounting to an article of faith, an absolute conviction, a reality as glittering as the sun. And I did create that belief that Arsène Lupin would escape, that

Arsène Lupin would not be present at his trial. And when you gave your evidence and said: "That man is not Arsène Lupin," everybody was prepared to believe you. Had one person doubted it, had any one uttered this simple restriction: Suppose it is Arsène Lupin?—from that moment, I was lost. If anyone had scrutinized my face, not imbued with the idea that I was not Arsène Lupin, as you and the others did at my trial, but with the idea that I might be Arsène Lupin; then, despite all my precautions, I should have been recognized. But I had no fear. Logically, psychologically, no once could entertain the idea that I was Arsène Lupin."

He grasped Ganimard's hand.

"Come, Ganimard, confess that on the Wednesday after our conversation in the prison de la Santé, you expected me at your house at four o'clock, exactly as I said I would go."

"And your prison-van?" said Ganimard, evading the question.

"A bluff! Some of my friends secured that old unused van and wished to make the attempt. But I considered it impractical without the concurrence of a number of unusual circumstances. However, I found it useful to carry out that attempted escape and give it the widest publicity. An audaciously planned escape, though not completed, gave to the succeeding one the character of reality simply by anticipation."

"So that the cigar...."

"Hollowed by myself, as well as the knife."

"And the letters?"

"Written by me."

"And the mysterious correspondent?"

"Did not exist."

Ganimard reflected a moment, then said:

"When the anthropological service had Baudru's case under consideration, why did they not perceive that his measurements coincided with those of Arsène Lupin?"

"My measurements are not in existence."

"Indeed!"

"At least, they are false. I have given considerable attention to that question. In the first place, the Bertillon system records the visible marks of identification—and you have seen that they are not infallible—and, after that, the measurements of the head, the fingers, the ears, etc. Of course, such measurements are more or less infallible."

"Absolutely."

"No; but it costs money to get around them. Before we

left America, one of the employees of the service there accepted so much money to insert false figures in my measurements. Consequently, Baudru's measurements should not agree with those of Arsène Lupin."

After a short silence, Ganimard asked:

"What are you going to do now?"

"Now," replied Lupin, "I am going to take a rest, enjoy the best of food and drink and gradually recover my former healthy condition. It is all very well to become Baudru or some other person, on occasion, and to change your personality as you do your shirt, but you soon grow weary of the change. I feel exactly as I imagine the man who lost his shadow must have felt, and I shall be glad to be Arsène Lupin once more."

He walked to and fro for a few minutes, then, stopping in front of Ganimard, he said:

"You have nothing more to say, I suppose?"

"Yes. I should like to know if you intend to reveal the true state of facts connected with your escape. The mistake that I made—"

"Oh! no one will ever know that it was Arsène Lupin who was discharged. It is to my own interest to surround myself with mystery, and therefore I shall permit my escape to retain its almost miraculous character. So, have no fear on that score, my dear friend. I shall say nothing. And now, good-bye. I am going out to dinner this evening, and have only sufficient time to dress."

"I though you wanted a rest."

"Ah! there are duties to society that one cannot avoid. To-morrow, I shall rest."

"Where do you dine to-night?"

"With the British Ambassador!"

ABOUT THE AUTHOR

Maurice Leblanc dropped out of law school to become a writer and move to Paris. His early works were critically acclaimed but had little commercial success. It is believed an editor asked him to write a French response to Sherlock Holmes and the instantly popular gentlemen thief Arsène Lupin was born.

ABOUT THE COVER

The image on the cover is adapted from the book cover from the 1910 french edition of "Arsène Lupin contre Herlock Sholmès".

MORE BOOKS AT:

superlargeprint.com

KEEP ON READING!

This book is set in a font designed by Abelardo Gonzalez called OpenDyslexic

ISBN 9798748174558

Printed in Great Britain
by Amazon